CITIZENSHIP AND IMMIGRATION

FOUNDATIONS OF DEMOCRACY

CITIZENSHIP AND IMMIGRATION

Author and Series Advisor
Tom Lansford
Professor of Political Science
University of Southern Mississippi, Gulf Coast

MASON CREST

Mason Crest
450 Parkway Drive, Suite D
Broomall, PA 19008
www.masoncrest.com

MTM Publishing, Inc.
435 West 23rd Street, #8C
New York, NY 10011
www.mtmpublishing.com

President: Valerie Tomaselli
Vice President, Book Development: Hilary Poole
Designer: Annemarie Redmond
Copyeditor: Peter Jaskowiak
Editorial Assistant: Andrea St. Aubin

Series ISBN: 978-1-4222-3625-3
Hardback ISBN: 978-1-4222-3626-0
E-Book ISBN: 978-1-4222-8270-0

Library of Congress Cataloging-in-Publication Data
Names: Lansford, Tom, author.
Title: Citizenship and immigration / by Tom Lansford.
Description: Broomall, PA: Mason Crest, 2017. | Series: Foundations of
   democracy | Includes index.
Identifiers: LCCN 2016004305 | ISBN 9781422236260 (hardback) | ISBN
   9781422236253 (series) | ISBN 9781422282700 (ebook)
Subjects: LCSH: Citizenship—Juvenile literature. | Emigration and
   immigration—Juvenile literature.
Classification: LCC JF801 .L358 2017 | DDC 325/.1—dc23
LC record available at https://lccn.loc.gov/2016004305

Printed and bound in the United States of America.

First printing
9 8 7 6 5 4 3 2 1

TABLE OF CONTENTS

Key Icons to Look for:

Words to Understand: These words with their easy-to-understand definitions will increase the reader's understanding of the text, while building vocabulary skills.

Sidebars: This boxed material within the main text allows readers to build knowledge, gain insights, explore possibilities, and broaden their perspectives by weaving together additional information to provide realistic and holistic perspectives.

Research Projects: Readers are pointed toward areas of further inquiry connected to each chapter. Suggestions are provided for projects that encourage deeper research and analysis.

Text-Dependent Questions: These questions send the reader back to the text for more careful attention to the evidence presented there.

Series Glossary of Key Terms: This back-of-the-book glossary contains terminology used throughout the series. Words found here increase the reader's ability to read and comprehend higher-level books and articles in this field.

Iraqi women at a political rally in 2010, in advance of the country's parliamentary elections.

SERIES INTRODUCTION

Democracy is a form of government in which the people hold all or most of the political power. In democracies, government officials are expected to take actions and implement policies that reflect the will of the majority of the citizenry. In other political systems, the rulers generally rule for their own benefit, or at least they usually put their own interests first. This results in deep differences between the rulers and the average citizen. In undemocratic states, elites enjoy far more privileges and advantages than the average citizen. Indeed, autocratic governments are often created to exploit the average citizen.

Elections allow citizens to choose representatives to make choices for them, and under some circumstances to decide major issues themselves. Yet democracy is much more than campaigns and elections. Many nations conduct elections but are not democratic. True democracy is dependent on a range of freedoms for its citizenry, and it simultaneously exists to protect and enhance those freedoms. At its best, democracy ensures that elites, average citizens, and even groups on the margins of society all have the same rights, privileges, and opportunities. The components of democracy have changed over time as individuals and groups have struggled to expand equality. In doing so, the very notion of what makes up a democracy has evolved. The volumes in this series examine the core freedoms that form the foundation of modern democracy.

Citizenship and Immigration explores what it means to be a citizen in a democracy. The principles of democracy are based on equality, liberty, and government by the consent of the people. Equality means that all citizens have the same rights and responsibilities. Democracies have struggled to integrate all groups and ensure full equality. Citizenship in a democracy is the formal recognition that a person is a member of the country's political community. Modern democracies have faced profound debates over immigration, especially how many people to admit to the country and what rights to confer on immigrants who are not citizens.

Challenges have also emerged within democracies over how to ensure disadvantaged groups enjoy full equality with the majority, or traditionally dominant, populations. While outdated legal or political barriers have been mostly removed, democracies still struggle to overcome cultural or economic impediments to equality. *Gender Equality and Identity Rights* analyzes why gender equality has proven especially challenging, requiring political, economic, and cultural reforms. Concurrently, *Religious, Cultural, and Minority Rights* surveys the efforts that democracies have undertaken to integrate disadvantaged groups into the political, economic, and social mainstream.

A free and unfettered media provides an important check on government power and ensures an informed citizenry. The importance of free expression and a free press are detailed in *Speech, Media, and Protest,* while *Employment and Workers' Rights* provides readers with an overview of the importance of economic liberty and the ways in which employment and workers' rights reinforce equality by guaranteeing opportunity.

The maintenance of both liberty and equality requires a legal system in which the police are constrained by the rule of law. This means that security officials understand and respect the rights of individuals and groups and use their power in a manner that benefits communities, not represses them. While this is the ideal, legal systems continue to struggle to achieve equality, especially among disadvantaged groups. These topics form the core of *Justice, Policing, and the Rule of Law.*

Corruption and Transparency examines the greatest danger to democracy: corruption. Corruption can undermine people's faith in government and erode equality. Transparency, or open government, provides the best means to prevent corruption by ensuring that the decisions and actions of officials are easily understood.

As discussed in *Political Participation and Voting Rights,* a government of the people requires its citizens to provide regular input on policies and decisions through consultations and voting. Despite the importance of voting, the history of democracies has been marked by the struggle to expand voting rights. Many groups, including women, only gained the right to vote in the last century, and continue to be underrepresented in political office.

Ultimately, all of the foundations of democracy are interrelated. Equality ensures liberty, while liberty helps maintain equality. Meanwhile, both are necessary for a government by consent to be effective and lasting. Within a democracy, all people must be treated equally and be able to enjoy the full range of liberties of the country, including rights such as free speech, religion, and voting.

—Tom Lansford

CHAPTER ONE

CITIZENSHIP

 ## WORDS TO UNDERSTAND

citizenship: formal recognition that an individual is a member of a political community.

democracy: a political system in which citizens hold all or most political power.

dual citizenship: being a full citizen of two or more countries.

felon: someone who has been convicted of a serious crime (a felony), such as murder, burglary, kidnapping, and treason.

naturalization: the legal process by which a resident noncitizen becomes a citizen of a country.

treason: the betrayal of one's country.

G overnments typically divide their population into two groups, citizens and noncitizens. A citizen is a formal member of a political system, such as a country, state, or province, or even a city or town. **Citizenship** confers both rights and responsibilities on individuals. Citizens owe their loyalty to their government, and in exchange for that allegiance, they receive a range of benefits. They are also

Shoppers on Takeshita Street, in Tokyo. Japan has one the highest rates of citizenship in the world.

expected to participate in governance through a variety of activities, ranging from paying taxes to voting. Noncitizens may reside in a political community, but they often do not have the same economic, political, or social rights as the citizens of that area.

Within any country, the majority of the populace are citizens. For instance, 92.3 percent of the people who live in Germany are citizens, as are 87.1 percent of those in the United States, while Japan has one of the highest rates of citizenship in the world at 98.8 percent. The most common way to obtain citizenship is through birth. Countries around the globe usually confer citizenship on the children of their citizens. In some instances, when one parent is from one country, but the other parent is from a different country, their children may be granted **dual citizenship**. Some nations forbid dual citizenship and require children to renounce the citizenship of other countries when they turn 18.

Citizenship may be restricted for residents who live in a country they were not born in. Countries may impose conditions before an individual can gain citizenship. Common conditions include residency for a specific period of time and no history of criminal activity.

RIGHTS AND RESPONSIBILITIES

Citizenship comes with both rights and responsibilities. Citizens have access to the full range of a nation's civil liberties, which are legal protections against unwarranted government interference or action, such as arbitrary arrest or the indiscriminate confiscation of property. Common civil liberties include freedom of religion, free speech, and the right to a fair trial. In addition, citizenship usually allows individuals to work in restricted occupations closed to noncitizens. For instance, most nations restrict the ability of noncitizens to work in national security fields such as weapons research and design.

Citizenship is a vital component of **democracy**. Indeed, citizens are the building blocks of democratic governments. Governments rely on citizens to help make decisions about major issues and to run the country. Citizenship also grants people the right to seek elected office. One of the key rights of any citizen is the ability to vote in elections. All countries restrict voting by noncitizens in elections, with some notable exceptions.

COMPULSORY VOTING AROUND THE WORLD

Country	Age of eligibility for mandatory voting	Country	Age of eligibility for mandatory voting
Argentina	18	Honduras	18
Australia	18	Lebanon	21
Belgium	18	Luxembourg	18
Bolivia	18	Mexico	18
Brazil	18	Nauru	20
Congo, Democratic Republic of the	18	Panama	18
Costa Rica	18	Paraguay	18
Dominican Republic	18	Peru	18
Ecuador	18	Singapore	21
Egypt	18	Thailand	18
Greece	18	Uruguay	18

Source: *CIA World Factbook*. "Suffrage." https://www.cia.gov/library/publications/the-world-factbook/fields/2123.html.

For instance, countries in Western Europe allow noncitizens to vote in local elections once they have lived in an area for a certain period of time. Furthermore, many members of the Commonwealth of Nations, an organization of former colonies of the United Kingdom, permit British citizens to vote in their elections.

While voting is considered a right, it is also seen as a responsibility. Democratic governments need citizens to cast ballots in order to ensure the legitimacy of elections. Twenty-two nations even require citizens to vote or face penalties such as fines—an obligation known as compulsory voting (see table). For example, failure to vote in Australia can result in a $26 fine.

Citizenship also comes with a range of other responsibilities. Citizens are expected to obey a nation's laws and pay their taxes. They are also often required to serve on juries in legal cases. Citizens have a duty to defend their country by serving in the military when required. Many countries still have compulsory military service, known as conscription, whereby citizens must serve a specific period in the national armed forces. Usually the compulsory military service lasts one to two years and begins after someone turns 18. Countries ranging from Austria to Brazil to Israel to South Korea continue to have conscription, although many nations also allow alternative forms of national service. With the exception of Israel, only men are subject to conscription in peacetime. Alternatives to conscription might be public service, teaching, or even working on construction projects. Those countries without conscription retain the authority to force citizens to join the military during times of national emergency.

Soldiers at Israel's School of Infantry Professions take a break during a drill. Israel is one of the few countries in the world where military service is compulsory for both men and women.

Besides the formal responsibilities of citizenship, countries also expect their citizens to be active members of their local communities. Governments want their citizens to stay informed of local and national issues and participate in public meetings and events. Finally, democratic systems require that citizens respect the rights and views of others, even if they disagree with those opinions.

BECOMING A CITIZEN

Because citizenship binds individuals to their government, countries offer various ways for residents to become citizens. As noted earlier, most people gain citizenship through their parents. In addition, some countries grant citizenship to anyone born on their soil. All children born in the United States are automatically U.S. citizens; this is stipulated by the Fourteenth Amendment to the Constitution. Conversely, a small number of countries, including Myanmar (Burma) do not allow **naturalization**; citizenship is confined to those with at least one parent who is a citizen.

 ## CITIZENSHIP REQUIREMENTS IN ARGENTINA AND SPAIN

Naturalization is simple and straightforward in some nations, but it can be highly complicated in others. In Argentina, an applicant for naturalization must be 18 years old, a resident of the country for two years, and not have been in prison for more than three of the past five years. On the other hand, Spain requires prospective citizens to reside there for five years and become permanent residents. After an additional five years, one can then apply for citizenship, but you have to prove you are integrated into Spanish society by demonstrating, among other things, competency in the Spanish language and participation in Spanish cultural activities. You also have to provide a statement of good conduct from the police.

A memorial to the many people who fled Ireland during the famine of the mid 1800s.
To encourage Irish expatriates to return, Ireland has long had a policy in place that anyone
with at least one grandparent born in Ireland is welcome to apply for citizenship.

FELONS AND VOTING RIGHTS

Many nations restrict the rights of people who have been convicted of serious crimes. For instance, 48 of the 50 U.S. states restrict the voting rights of felons while they are in prison (Maine and Vermont are the exceptions). Felons permanently lose their voting rights in 11 U.S. states. However, most other democracies not only permit felons to vote, but they also have special programs to ensure that convicts may cast ballots while they are in prison. Such countries include Canada, France, Japan, and Peru.

A ballot box for an election in France in 2008.

Residents who are noncitizens may also go through a process known as naturalization to acquire citizenship. The naturalization process varies from country to country, but it generally requires an applicant to live continuously in a nation for a designated period of time and meet certain other requirements. Among Western European countries, the average residency threshold is five to seven years. Countries also often require the applicant to be fluent in one of the national languages and pass a citizenship exam. Applicants generally are disqualified if they are **felons** or have a substantial criminal record. To become a British citizen, an individual must have lived in the United Kingdom for a minimum of five years, demonstrate a proficiency in one of the nation's languages (English, Welsh, or Scottish Gaelic), and not be a felon. Applicants must also pass a test on British history, politics, and culture, known as the Life in the UK Test.

Some countries speed the naturalization process for the spouses of citizens. For example, in Japan, naturalization normally requires a minimum five-year period of residency. However, if the would-be citizen is married to someone who is already a citizen, the requirement is lowered to three years. In South Korea, the residency period is normally five years, but only two if someone is married to a citizen. Other nations expedite naturalization for people with special skills. While Russia normally mandates a five-year waiting period for naturalization, it can be reduced to one year for highly skilled individuals.

While noncitizens may be naturalized, people may lose their citizenship, or have their rights restricted, under certain circumstances. Citizenship may be revoked for those who have committed crimes against the state such as **treason**. Also, many countries forbid their citizens from joining the military service of another nation; someone who does so may forfeit citizenship in his country of origin. Finally, a number of countries do not recognize dual citizenship and require applicants to renounce any formal allegiance

Secretary of State Robert Gates (far left) and Valdas Adamkus, the president of Lithuania (far right), during a luncheon meeting at the White House in 2008. Adamkus was born in Lithuania but immigrated to the United States in 1949. He then gave up his U.S. citizenship to become president of his home country in 1998.

THE RISE OF DEMOCRACY

Democracy has spread rapidly to become the most common type of government in the world. Democracy expanded dramatically between 1990 and 2000, but declined slightly between 2000 and 2010.

Year	1970	1980	1990	2000	2010
Number of Democracies in the World	45	58	75	120	115

Source: "Democracy in the World." http://www.democracyw.com/2011/07/trend-of-democratic-countries-in-world.html.

to another nation. Otherwise, a person would face the loss of citizenship. A small number of countries, such as Costa Rica, never revoke citizenship under any circumstances. People who lack formal citizenship are known as stateless persons.

TEXT-DEPENDENT QUESTIONS

1. How do most people gain citizenship?
2. What are the main responsibilities of citizens?
3. What are the three most common reasons people lose their citizenship?

RESEARCH PROJECTS

1. Research compulsory voting. Develop a chart or write a brief summary arguing either for or against the practice of requiring citizens to vote.
2. Research naturalization in the United States and one other country. Create a chart that highlights the similarities and differences in the processes in the two countries.

CHAPTER TWO

IMMIGRATION CATEGORIES

WORDS TO UNDERSTAND

assimilation: the process through which immigrants adopt the cultural, political, and social beliefs of a new nation.

chain immigration: the process by which noncitizen family members of a lawful immigrant or citizen are allowed to also immigrate.

deportation: the legal process whereby undocumented immigrants or those who have violated residency laws are forced to leave their new country.

guest workers: citizens of one country who have been granted permission to temporarily work in another nation.

undocumented immigrants: people who do not have the legal right to reside in a country because they entered the nation illegally or remained after their legal period of residency ended; sometimes also known as undocumented aliens.

Immigrants are people who permanently move from their home country to another nation. They are also sometimes referred to as aliens. Often, immigrants are seeking better lives for themselves and their families. They may also be fleeing conflict or strife. Since the 1990s, immigration has grown substantially. In 2014 the United Nations found that there were 232 million immigrants around the globe, or 3.2 percent of the world's population. That number rose from 154 million in 1990, and from 175 million in 2000.

THE UNIVERSAL DECLARATION OF HUMAN RIGHTS

The 1948 Universal Declaration of Human Rights (UDHR) endorsed the right of people to leave their home nation and seek asylum if necessary. According to Section 1 of Article 13 of the UDHR, "Everyone has the right to leave any country, including his own, and to return to his country." Meanwhile, Article 14, Section 1 declares that "Everyone has the right to seek and to enjoy in other countries asylum from persecution." The next section clarifies the allowable reasons for asylum: "This right may not be invoked in the case of prosecutions genuinely arising from non-political crimes or from acts contrary to the purposes and principles of the United Nations."

In 1949, First Lady Eleanor Roosevelt poses with an oversized copy of the UDHR translated into Spanish. Roosevelt was a central figure in the movement to write and ratify the agreement.

Immigrants often face a range of challenges in their new countries. They may have trouble with **assimilation**, and some nations have laws that restrict the rights of noncitizens. Naturalization provides a means for immigrants to become citizens in their new nations. However, naturalization requires immigrants to be residents of their new country for various periods of time, depending on the nation. Consequently, countries have a population of noncitizens. Some are awaiting citizenship, while others live in their new country without becoming a citizen. In some cases, the immigrants cannot meet the citizenship requirements. For instance, they may be unable or unwilling to learn a new language, they may have committed crimes that disqualify them, or they may simply wish to remain citizens of their home country out of loyalty or a desire to return one day. The result is that within any given country, there are residents or aliens who never become citizens.

ASYLUM SEEKERS

Asylum seekers are people who flee their native country because of political or social persecution. Sometimes known as refugees, they have a right to apply for asylum, or temporary sanctuary, in another country. The right of asylum is an ancient one that was created to provide safe places for people facing persecution in their homeland. The right of asylum was recognized internationally by the United Nations in 1948 through the Universal Declaration of Human Rights. To qualify as an asylum seeker, a person must file a formal request for sanctuary with a national government or an international organization such as the United Nations. If their request is granted, asylum seekers are often reclassified as refugees, meaning they are temporary residents of a nation who are waiting for conditions to improve so that they may return to their home.

The number of people seeking asylum around the world has increased as the number of conflicts and wars have grown. In 2015 there were more than 60 ongoing conflicts around the world, the majority of which were civil wars, in which different groups were fighting each other within the borders of a given country. Countries near active conflicts or wars often have large influxes of asylum seekers. For instance, because of the war in

Syrian refugees at a camp in Suruc, Turkey, in 2015.

Afghanistan, there are more than 1.6 million refugees in Pakistan. By 2015 there were more than 19.5 million asylum seekers worldwide.

Asylum seekers and refugees often pose special challenges for their host countries. Many have experienced significant trauma and have physical and mental wounds that strain the medical and mental health resources of their homes. Also, because many refugees want to return to their homes, there is less incentive to assimilate into their host country's society or economy. However, nations are obligated to take these asylum seekers in and provide for them until their home countries stabilize. This obligation can become extraordinarily complicated. For example, the civil war in Syria, which began in 2011, had produced an estimated 4 million refugees by 2015. Large numbers of these refugees sought asylum in wealthy countries far away from the conflict, such as Germany or Sweden. This led to a global debate over the duty of states to accommodate refugees from foreign conflicts.

REFUGEE CAMPS

Refugees fleeing strife or conflict may be housed a refugee camp. These camps are temporary facilities operated by a host country or an international organization such as the United Nations. These camps may also house immigrants that are apprehended attempting to illegally enter a nation. In 2015 the United Nations estimated there were more than 18 million refugees around the globe, including 5.1 million that were housed in 60 major refugee camps in the Middle East. More than half the world's refugees originated in Asia, with another third from Africa. Although the camps are supposed to be temporary, many have been in existence for decades. The refugees often find themselves as essentially stateless people who cannot return to their homes, but also cannot be assimilated into their host countries.

A Somali refugee camp in Eritrea, just west of the city of Massawa, 2011.

GUEST WORKERS

Another group of temporary immigrants is **guest workers**. Some countries, such as Japan, have declining populations and need additional workers to keep their economies going. Other nations permit guest workers because they have shortages of native-born workers in specific occupations. For example, because agricultural work tends to be low-paying and physically difficult, some countries face problems finding enough employees to fill those jobs. To fill that need, guest workers may be allowed in to undertake agricultural harvests. Such workers typically stay in their host countries for only a few months before returning home. At the other end of the spectrum, some countries seek out highly skilled workers in areas such as computer programing or graphic design. Guest workers travel to new countries for higher pay and better working conditions.

Countries with guest worker programs highly regulate the use of these noncitizen employees. Guest workers are typically required to sign an agreement that regulates how much they may be paid, how long they may stay in the country, and sometimes where they may live. Guest workers seldom have the same rights as citizens of their host countries. They may also face hostility by those who argue that these programs take jobs away from citizens.

 ## INTERNATIONAL STUDENTS

Many countries open their schools and colleges to foreign students. These international students broaden and enrich the educational experience of native students. In addition, foreign students who learn valuable skills may stay in their host country and work in high-demand occupations such as engineering or medicine. International students who return to their home countries bring new perspectives and skills to their societies. The number of international college students more than doubled from 2000 to 2011, rising from 2.1 million to 4.5 million, and then increasing to more than 5 million by 2014. The United States is largest destination for international students, with about 20 percent of the world's total.

An agricultural worker from Mexico trims plants on a farm in Kern County, California.

A neighborhood in Qatar that is home to the country's many Nepalese guest workers.

UNDOCUMENTED IMMIGRANTS

Some countries do not have guest worker programs. Those that do, limit the number of people who may participate in these initiatives. However, the lure of higher pay and better working conditions may prompt people to immigrate illegally. In other cases, people who are unable to qualify for asylum still leave their home to avoid persecution or harassment. Sometimes people are allowed in a country for short periods of time to study, work, or visit relatives, after which they decide to remain illegally. The result is a population of **undocumented immigrants**, especially in wealthier nations. Estimates are that 15 to 20 percent of all immigrants in the world are undocumented.

Since undocumented immigrants are in a country illegally, they face a range of challenges. Employers may take advantage of them by underpaying them or even denying them their wages. Landlords may overcharge them for rent. The immigrants are usually unwilling to contact the police or other authorities for fear of being subject to **deportation**. Undocumented immigrants also face difficulties in enrolling in school or accessing health care and other social services.

RESTRICTIONS ON IMMIGRATION

Most countries restrict immigration and have limitations on guest worker programs. These restrictions may be designed to prevent immigration by undesirable individuals, such as criminals or those with dangerous diseases. Limitations may also be in place to prevent large numbers of immigrants from straining educational or social programs, or to protect the jobs of citizens in certain industries. For instance, war and conflict in the Middle East and Africa led to a wave of undocumented immigrants to Europe in the second decade of the 21st century. The number of undocumented immigrants in Greece rose from about 20,000 in 2005 to 500,000 in 2014. In response, countries across Europe sought to restrict the ability of undocumented immigrants to reach their borders, including tripling the amount spent on patrols in the Mediterranean Sea to intercept those trying to cross the waters to reach Europe.

One result is that the immigration process for most countries can be lengthy and expensive. Extensive paperwork is often required. Governments want immigrants, but they seek those that can assimilate and contribute to the broader society. However, **chain immigration**, which allows family members of new citizens to also immigrate, can complicate efforts to control the total number of new immigrants. Nations constantly struggle to find a balance between welcoming new immigrants and limiting the number of new arrivals to an appropriate amount. One of the central issues in the immigration debate is the economic impact of new residents.

TEXT-DEPENDENT QUESTIONS

1. What are the two main reasons people immigrate to new countries?
2. Why do countries have guest worker programs?
3. What are the main challenges faced by undocumented immigrants?

RESEARCH PROJECTS

1. Research the rise of global immigration. What factors have led to an increase in immigration? What countries have the most immigrants? Why?
2. Research guest worker programs. Write a brief report that identifies the main arguments for and against such initiatives. Choose a country with a guest worker program and include a summary of how well that program operates.

CHAPTER THREE

THE ECONOMICS OF IMMIGRATION

 ## WORDS TO UNDERSTAND

bilingual: the ability to fluently speak and understand two languages.

developing countries: nations that are not as economically advanced as others, and generally have a lower standard of living than more advanced economies.

expatriate: someone who chooses to reside in a country other than his or her nation of birth.

remittances: money transfers from individuals in one country to individuals in another country, typically sent to families and friends.

underground ("gray") economy: economic activities that are not taxed or monitored by the government.

Many nations encourage immigration because new citizens may improve the country in a range of ways. Immigrants expand the workforce by providing new laborers. This is especially important for countries with declining or aging populations. For instance, the average age is 44 in Austria, 41 in Canada, and 46 in both Germany and Japan. Immigrants tend to be younger than the general population, and therefore have longer working lives ahead of them than the existing population. Younger workers also tend to spend more and buy more, and they pay taxes on the goods and services they purchase. All of this stimulates the economy. For instance, Canada has a large immigrant community (almost 20 percent of its population was born overseas), and immigration has been estimated to have increased the country's economy by almost 2 percent annually.

Immigrants are also often more mobile than the native population, and they are therefore more willing to move to areas that need workers. As a result of immigration, employers are able to keep wages lower than they would otherwise, and this keeps prices lower for consumers. This is especially true in fields such as agriculture.

Not all immigrants engage in low-wage jobs, however. Countries can target highly skilled immigrants to reduce shortages in high-demand occupations. Also, some immigrants with advanced degrees—in medicine or engineering, for example—seek higher pay and a better standard of living in wealthier countries. Studies of immigration to developed countries have found that immigrants are more likely to have advanced

 DEVELOPING COUNTRIES

The majority of the world's nations are identified as developing countries: in 2016, the World Bank put 135 out of 194 nations in this category. The majority of developing countries have annual average incomes of less than $4,200. In many countries, the average annual income is less than $1,000. The people of Timor-Leste, Malawi, and Somalia have average annual incomes of less than $600. In contrast, Qatar has the world's highest annual per person income, at $93,397. Most immigrants in the world come from developing states. Some estimates are that 85 percent of immigrants are from developing countries.

The Gates of Harmonious Interest, built in China and erected in Victoria, British Columbia. About 20 percent of Canada's population are immigrants.

degrees than the native population. In 2011, for instance, 38 percent of immigrants to the United Kingdom had college degrees, compared with just 21 percent of the native-born population.

Immigrants also bring different perspectives and traditions to their new homes. This helps cultures grow and stay vibrant by adding new elements. For instance, curry, an Indian spice, has become commonplace in the United Kingdom. In the United States, salsa has replaced ketchup as the most commonly used condiment.

Indian, Pakistani, and Bangladeshi shops along Brick Lane in London.

These minor examples demonstrate how immigrants can influence the broader culture of their new homes.

THE COSTS OF IMMIGRATION

Immigration is not without its costs or problems. Immigrants who are willing to work for lower pay than the native population cause wages to stagnate or even decrease. Immigrants may also increase competition for existing jobs, leading to charges that they are taking employment away from the native-born population. Employers may find it cheaper to hire workers from overseas, rather than employ native-born workers. In 2015, for example, it was revealed that the Walt Disney Company had replaced 250 U.S. employees with temporary workers from overseas. These new workers were paid less for the same work.

New immigrants may increase the cost of some social services, such as education. Elementary and secondary education is considered a right. However, governments face challenges in educating immigrant children who speak a different language or who have different educational backgrounds. Opponents of wide-scale immigration assert that undocumented immigrants do not pay their fair share of taxes, since they often work in the **underground ("gray") economy.**

While some view immigration as beneficial to a nation's culture and traditions, others argue that new values or preferences weaken society. In France, for instance, the majority of the native population is Christian (80 percent of the population is Catholic). Recent immigration has increased the percentage of the people who are Muslims to 7.5 percent. The increase in Muslims has led to tensions over the practice of religion in schools and public spaces in France. In 2010, France banned wearing religious veils in public if they covered a women's face. The veil, or *niqāb,* is common among some sects of Islam.

One category of immigrants is increasingly posing a large dilemma for countries. A growing number of older **expatriates** are choosing to retire overseas. These retirees look

A woman wearing a niqāb sits on Parliament Hill in Ottawa, Ontario.

for countries with a lower cost of living so that their pensions and savings have more value. For instance, it is estimated that more than 25,000 U.S. retirees have moved to Costa Rica. These expatriates are transferring money from their home countries to their new homes.

REMITTANCES

A significant portion of modern immigrants come from **developing countries**. These migrants often seek economic opportunities in more developed states. Often they use

THE ECONOMIC IMPACT OF IMMIGRATION ON SOCIAL WELFARE PROGRAMS

Social welfare programs are initiatives to provide economic and other assistance to needy individuals and families. Providing social welfare benefits to immigrants, especially undocumented immigrants, is a controversial subject in many nations. Critics argue that immigrants proportionately receive more benefits from social welfare initiatives than the native population. Part of their argument is that immigrants have often not been in the country long enough to have paid an appropriate amount of taxes to cover the costs of social benefits. However, studies from a range of countries have found that recent immigrants use social welfare programs at a lower rate than the general population.

There are several reasons for this. First, new immigrants may not understand how to access benefits or know which programs they are eligible for. Second, immigrants may not meet eligibility requirements for programs because of the length of time they have been in a country or their residency status. Furthermore, undocumented immigrants are generally not entitled to social welfare benefits in most countries. Third, immigrants are often younger than the general population, and are therefore less likely to use medical services and more likely to be employed. This is especially true in Europe and the United States.

A busy waiting room at a hospital. The usage of social services by immigrants is a controversial aspect of the immigration debate.

WORLDWIDE REMITTANCES

Remittances can be a major source of income for many people in developing countries. Remittances often exceed the amount of official assistance that poorer countries receive from organizations such as the United Nations or the World Bank, or from more wealthy countries. In eight countries—Tajikistan, Liberia, Kyrgyzstan, Lesotho, Moldova, Nepal, Samoa, and Haiti—remittances make up more than 20 percent of the nation's total economy. Remittances are especially important during emergencies or periods of economic disruption. Senders can adjust their contributions quickly, making remittances more flexible than traditional loans from banks. There are potential problems with remittances, however. For instance, they are not as permanent as other forms of income. If someone who sends remittances losses his or her job, it affects not only that person, but also those who are receiving the remittances overseas. Following the 2008 global financial crisis, worldwide remittances declined by 6 percent as some immigrants in developed states lost their jobs of faced financial hardships.

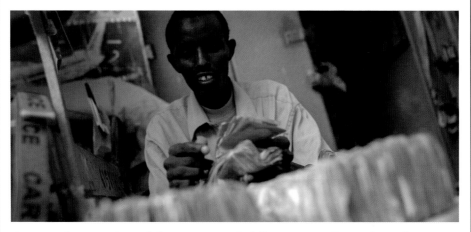

A money-changer in Mogadishu counts Somali shilling notes. Millions of Somalians depend on remittances from relatives abroad.

their time in another country to send **remittances** home to family members or loved ones. Remittances from wealthy countries can be an important source of income for family members living in poorer nations. Although they are difficult to track, it was estimated in 2014 that remittances to developing countries totaled more than $530 billion.

Remittances provide an important source of income for developing nations. The money helps families and serves as a means of direct economic investment. For instance, remittances could supply the money necessary to start a business or purchase a home. According to the Pew Research Center, in 2012, India was the largest recipient of remittances, taking in more than $69.4 billion. Of that, $15.7 billion was sent to India from the United Arab Emirates.

While remittances benefit developing countries, they remove money from the economies of the more developed nations. Money that could have been spent in Germany or Japan is instead sent to Turkey or the Philippines. In 2012 the United States was the largest source of remittances, sending more than $124.3 billion to other countries. Mexico was the largest recipient of U.S. remittances, at $22.8 billion.

EDUCATION

All developed, democratic nations view education as a right. However, there are two approaches to immigrant education, especially with regard to undocumented immigration. One line of thinking asserts that by putting additional resources into educating immigrants, societies are investing not only in the future of the individual student, but also in the future of the country itself, by producing more educated and skilled workers. On the other hand, some argue that undocumented immigrants undermine the educational system by soaking up resources. These costs include **bilingual** instruction at the primary and secondary levels and the expenses associated with college tuition.

Countries such as Argentina or Chile require instruction in Spanish, while most Western European states require bilingual education (and provide special accommodations for students whose primary language is not one of those taught by the educational institution). Issues such as educational costs have led to dramatic escalations in the debates over citizenship and immigration.

TEXT-DEPENDENT QUESTIONS:

1. What are some ways in which immigrants are often different from the native-born population?
2. What are potential problems with remittances for developed countries?
3. How can immigration add additional costs to an educational system?

RESEARCH PROJECTS

1. Chose a developing country and research that nation's economy and standard of living. Create a chart that compares the developing country with your own nation.
2. Research the economics of immigration in a country such as the United States, France, or the United Kingdom. Write a brief comparison of the main costs and benefits of immigration to that nation.

CHAPTER FOUR

IMMIGRATION POLITICS

 ## WORDS TO UNDERSTAND

hate crimes: criminal acts against people because of their race, ethnicity, religion, or nationality.

homogenous: a region or nation where most people have the same ethnicity, language, religion, customs, and traditions.

minority group: a group within a larger society that is different ethnically, racially, culturally, or in terms of religion.

political party: an organization of like-minded people that seeks to control or influence government and the policy process.

As the number of immigrants has increased around the world, debates have emerged within democratic countries over issues such as naturalization and the status of undocumented immigrants. In some instances, countries have made it easier for immigrants to become citizens. Some Western European nations have used the naturalization process to better integrate immigrants. These governments assume a significant amount of the responsibility for ensuring immigrants assimilate into the broader society. Other nations, including the United States, continue to place the majority of the burden of assimilation on the immigrant, making it an individual responsibility of the potential citizen.

The main incentive for nations to ease requirements for citizenship has been the presence of noncitizen residents. Countries want these groups to assimilate and become citizens. Immigrants typically face more challenges in **homogenous** nations. Migrants

A festival in Kvinesdal, Norway. Kvinesdal is known as an "American village" due to the large number of American immigrants who live there.

HOMOGENOUS NATIONS AND DIVERSE NATIONS

Japan and South Korea are among the most homogenous countries in the world, with populations that are more than 96 percent the same in terms of ethnicity, language, and culture. Other notably homogenous nations include Australia and a number of European nations, including Norway, Portugal, and Sweden. The most diverse nations in the world are all in Africa. For instance, Togo has 37 distinct tribal groups, each speaking one of more than 30 different languages (the official language is French—Togo was once a colony of France). Other nations with highly diverse populations are Canada, Mexico, and Brazil.

A traditional music performance in Kara, Togo. With 37 different tribes, Togo is one of the most diverse countries on Earth.

may be members of **minority groups** who may dress differently or speak a different language. Assimilation and citizenship provide a pathway to better integrate these residents into the broader society.

Since the 1990s, a number of nations have reduced their residency requirements for naturalization. In addition, countries have increased classes and educational programs

THE EUROPEAN UNION AND IMMIGRATION

The European Union (EU) is a political and economic organization of 28 European nations and more than 500 million people. In 1995, seven member countries of the EU removed internal borders, which allowed their citizens to freely travel or move to other nations without prior permission. As new countries joined the EU, they also eliminated restrictions on the movement of citizens of the EU. Nations in the EU now generally have two legal approaches to immigration and citizenship. One covers citizens of other EU states, while there are separate rules and regulations for migrants from non-EU countries. For instance, citizens of other EU nations do not need permission to move to Portugal, although they do have to register with the local government. However, a non-EU citizen must gain approval from the Portuguese Immigration Service before they move to the country. Germany and the United Kingdom have the largest number of migrants from other EU nations, while the country with the most immigrants going to other nations is Poland. Citizens from four non-EU countries—Iceland, Liechtenstein, Norway, and Switzerland—are also allowed to move about freely within the EU.

The flag of the European Union.

designed to help immigrants assimilate and, if they choose, become citizens. For instance, Norwegian law mandates that immigrants between the ages of 16 and 55 have a right and duty to complete 300 hours of free language instruction. After the initial classes, noncitizens may apply for up to an additional 2,400 hours of free language training. New immigrants also receive 50 hours of instruction in Norwegian social studies, so that they can better understand the country and its culture. Central to these initiatives is the idea that immigrants have an obligation to learn about their new country, and that they also have a right to assistance in the assimilation process.

IMMIGRATION REFORM

Around the globe, nations are making it easier for immigrants to become citizens. In some cases, however, governments are also making it more difficult to immigrate. One result is that it is less difficult for highly skilled people to move to, and become citizens of, new countries. For example, Japan has adopted a point-based immigration system. Skills such as advanced degrees or professional experience earn potential immigrants additional points on their immigration applications and speed approval. Other countries have reduced the process time for all applicants seeking to immigrate; Norway cut its maximum immigrant review period from two years to one. Quick approval for immigration is especially important in light of the wait periods that exist in some countries. In the United States, potential migrants may have to wait as long as 20 years for approval to immigrate because of limits on immigration. In 2014 there were 8.7 million people on waiting lists to immigrate to the United States.

Among the reforms that make it easier for immigrants to become citizens has been the abolition of requirements that resident aliens have a job. In 2006, for example, Norway and Portugal ended requirements that applicants for citizenship be permanently employed. Some countries, including Belgium, France, and Luxembourg, have cut the fees associated with naturalization.

A bronze statue in Kepaniwai Heritage Gardens in Maui, Hawaii. The statue commemorates the Japanse workers who immigrated to Hawaii to work the sugarcane fields in the late 19th century.

NONCITIZEN RIGHTS

In the past, immigrants typically had few rights in their new nations. It was not until residents became citizens that they enjoyed the full range of rights and liberties of their new country. Noncitizens still have fewer rights than citizens, but a number of nations have dramatically increased the civil liberties of noncitizens. As noted in a previous chapter, some nations now give resident noncitizens the right to vote in certain elections. In Japan, noncitizens are even able elect representatives to serve on special councils that work for their benefit on economic and social issues. Nations also grant noncitizen residents rights to social services such as education or health care.

Noncitizen rights may at times be restricted. For instance, many nations allow international students to attend a college or university, but they limit the student's ability to get a job while they are in the country, or impose restrictions on the amount of income they may earn. Nonstudent immigrants or residents may work in their new countries, but they usually have to have permission. German law requires immigrants to obtain permission for employment before they move to the country. Also, with the exception of some high-skilled occupations, immigrants are forbidden from accepting a job for which a suitable German worker is available.

ANTI-IMMIGRANT GROUPS

Within any country, there are groups opposed to immigration for various reasons. Some people are afraid that immigrants will change the culture of their nation. Since immigrants may have different traditions or religious beliefs, their presence may be perceived as a threat to existing social systems and values. While some might welcome a new restaurant with cuisine from another country in their neighborhood, others are upset over these types of changes. Sometimes immigrants are targets of **hate crimes**. Since around 2005, several countries in Europe have experienced a significant rise in violence against immigrants.

Opposition to immigrants has led to the rise of new **political parties** and groups. Anti-immigrant political parties have increased their support in many nations in Western Europe. In the United Kingdom, Denmark, Finland, and Sweden, anti-immigrant parties have significantly bolstered their support and their votes in recent elections. The anti-immigrant Sweden Democrats Party placed third out of nine major parties in national elections in Sweden in 2014; the Sweden Democrats pledged to cut immigration by 90 percent. These parties generally seek to limit immigration and make it more difficult for noncitizens to become citizens. They also promise to deport undocumented immigrants.

One issue that has fueled the rise of anti-immigrant parties has been crime. Some criminals and criminal gangs have immigrated to new countries. In the United Kingdom, for instance, the number of convicts who were immigrants from Eastern European countries increased by 10 percent between 2011 and 2013. Another major issue behind the increase in anti-immigrant parties is border security.

 ## HATE CRIMES

The number of hate crimes against immigrants in Europe and Russia has increased dramatically, doubling between 2005 and 2015. Russia, Greece, Italy, and Spain had the largest increases in attacks. Some of the rise in violence has been directed at Muslims. Mosques have been attacked and vandalized, and Muslims dressed in traditional garb have been targeted in public places by anti-immigrant gangs. There has also been a rise in violence directed toward African immigrants, most noticeably in countries such as France, Italy, and Russia. Recently, even migrants from Eastern European nations have faced growing threats and attacks in Ireland and the United Kingdom. In response, many countries have strengthened their laws against hate crimes. For instance, the United Kingdom expanded the scope of its hate crime laws and bolstered penalties in 2011.

A rally in Sydney by the anti-Muslim group Reclaim Australia in April 2015.

TEXT-DEPENDENT QUESTIONS

1. What reforms have nations undertaken to make it easier for residents to become citizens?
2. What are some of the ways in which the rights of noncitizens rights may be different than citizens of a nation?
3. What types of policies do anti-immigrant parties support?

RESEARCH PROJECTS

1. Choose a country and research restrictions on immigration. Describe the restrictions in a report that explores how difficult it is for immigrants to move to that nation.
2. Research your nation's two main political parties. Write a brief report that compares the positions the two parties take on immigration, and create a chart that highlights the similarities and differences.

CHAPTER FIVE

BORDER SECURITY

 ## WORDS TO UNDERSTAND

amnesty: a formal reprieve or pardon for people accused or convicted of committing crimes.

drug trafficking: the cultivation, distribution, and sale of illicit drugs.

human rights: rights that everyone has, regardless of birthplace or citizenship.

illegal immigration: the movement of people from one nation to another without legal permission.

terrorism: the use of violence to achieve a political or religious goal.

Just as legal immigration has increased substantially since the 1990s, so has **illegal immigration** by undocumented immigrants. In 2014 there were an estimated 860,000 undocumented, or illegal, immigrants in the United Kingdom, 750,000 in Italy, and 11.4 million in the United States. Many of these undocumented immigrants have lived in their host countries for long periods of time. However, since they are in their particular country illegally, it is either very difficult or even impossible for them to become naturalized citizens. One approach some nations have used is to grant **amnesty** to undocumented immigrants, thereby providing a process by which people's residency can be legalized. In 2005, for instance, Spain provided 700,000 renewable work permits to illegal immigrants. To be eligible, residents had to demonstrate that they had a job and were paying taxes. The permits allowed the undocumented immigrants to become legal residents.

Other nations have tried to deal with undocumented residents by increasing fines and penalties for those caught. Japan has significantly increased punishments for illegal immigrants, who are now subject to up to three years imprisonment and a fine of $2,500. The result has been a dramatic decrease in the number of people immigrating there illegally, from an estimated 300,000 in 2000 to 150,000 by 2008. In Operation Mare Nostrum (see sidebar on page 50), Italy increased its naval patrols to intercept illegal

The Irish navy rescues a boat of migrants as part of Operation Triton.

OPERATION MARE NOSTRUM

In October 2013, the Italian government launched a major naval operation in response to a massive wave of immigration from North Africa. Dubbed "Mare Nostrum" (the Roman name for the Mediterranean Sea), the mission sought to rescue migrants at sea, many of whom were in flimsy boats that were unsuited to the rough sea. It also sought to apprehend smugglers. Drones and aircraft were used to identify migrant crafts. During the year-long effort, the Italian Navy rescued more than 150,000 migrants and transported them to refugee centers in Europe. Italian authorities also apprehended 330 smugglers. The operation was replaced by a smaller mission after other European countries declined an Italian request for funding to pay for the deployment, which cost $142 million.

migrants trying to enter the country from the sea. The enhanced patrols were designed to deter illegal immigrants, but also to rescue those in difficulty. However, the initiative cost the country $12 million per month.

Some undocumented immigrants were initially in their host country legally, but then overstayed their permitted length of residency. As an example, some international students either complete their education or drop out, and then decide to remain in their new country. Other people enter a country as tourists and simply try to stay instead of returning at the end of their visit. In other cases, people intentionally enter a country without permission.

Attempting to reach a new country without proper paperwork or permission can be highly dangerous. Illegal immigrants often have to travel hazardous routes across deserts or oceans. In 2012, at least 477 migrants died trying to cross the border from Mexico into the United States. That year, an estimated 1,000 died attempting to cross the Mediterranean Sea from North Africa to Europe.

SMUGGLING

In a growing number of countries, illegal immigration has become an issue in a broader debate over border security. Smuggling, the illicit movement of goods or people across borders, has been a problem for governments for centuries. Smugglers often sneak goods into a country to avoid paying taxes on the items, or because the item is illegal, such as illicit drugs.

Smugglers also illegally convey people across borders in exchange for payment or services. These criminals, or "coyotes," charge undocumented immigrants up to $5,000 to transport them across the border from Mexico to the United States. Women are often sexually abused for payment. Illegal immigrants from Asia are often charged more than $10,000 (the higher costs reflect the greater difficulty and distances involved in moving people from Asia). An estimated 55,000 people are smuggled into Europe each year by criminals who make an estimated $150 million from the immigrants.

The criminal organizations that smuggle people across borders often are also engaged in other types of illegal activity. Smugglers may also be involved in **drug**

ILLEGAL IMMIGRATION IN THE UNITED STATES

The United States has the largest number of illegal immigrants of any nation in the world. Estimates are that more than 3.5 percent of the U.S. population is in the country illegally. Almost 60 percent of undocumented immigrants in the country are from Mexico. There are also large numbers from El Salvador, Guatemala, and the Philippines. More than 2.8 million undocumented immigrants live in California, followed by 1.8 million in Texas, and 730,000 in Florida. About 53 percent are male, and more than 55 percent are under the age of 35. The majority of illegal immigrants work in either agriculture or construction.

One end of the border fence between the United States and Mexico, near Sasabe, Arizona.

trafficking. Increasingly, the criminal groups that smuggle people into the United States also move illegal drugs into the country. In addition, some people are smuggled into countries against their will and forced to engage in criminal activities. Human trafficking, the illegal movement of people for criminal activities, was a $96 billion illicit industry in 2014. Only drug trafficking brought in more cash, with an estimated value of more than $400 billion.

TERRORISM

The 21st century has witnessed an increase in global **terrorism**. Just between 2012 and 2013, deaths from terrorism increased more than 50 percent worldwide. The rise in political violence has heightened concerns that terrorists might be able to sneak into countries through routes used by smugglers. However, there have also been instances when terrorists were able to legally enter countries. For example, 16 of the 19 hijackers who participated in the September 11, 2001, terrorist attacks were able to enter the United States legally.

Concerns over terrorism have led to new efforts to improve border security throughout the world. From 2001 to 2009, the United States increased the number of border patrol agents from 9,800 to over 20,000. During the same period, the United States built fences along approximately 600 miles of the 2,000 mile-long U.S.–Mexico border. In 2015, when large numbers of undocumented migrants attempted to travel to the United Kingdom through a tunnel connecting the country with France, the British government spent $18.9 million to increase security.

Anti-immigrant political parties have highlighted the threat of terrorism as one of the key reasons to restrict immigration and increase border security. The potential for terrorism was one of the reasons cited by groups opposed to immigrants from Syria in 2015. However, supporters of immigration warn that tying terrorism and immigration together creates a culture of fear and hostility for both legal and illegal migrants. One consequence could be further increases in hate crimes.

EXPLOITATION

Because they are in a country illegally, undocumented immigrants are often targets for exploitation. These immigrants are often taken advantage of in areas such as employment and housing. In 2013 the European Union launched a major investigation into illegal labor practices across Europe. The investigators uncovered many instances of employees forced to work long hours for less pay than the law required. Undocumented immigrants were also often not paid back wages, and many worked in conditions that were unsafe. However, the aliens were reluctant to file formal complaints because of their immigration status. At the same time, undocumented immigrants may be forced to pay higher rents and accept substandard housing because they are hesitant to complain.

The exploitation of illegal immigrants presents governments with significant challenges. Countries do not have to grant undocumented immigrants the same rights

A rally in favor of immigration reform in Bakersfield, California. Undocumented laborers are at risk of exploitation because they are not able to report problems to authorities for fear of deportation.

HUNGARY'S BORDER

A large number of illegal immigrants have crossed into the Eastern European country of Hungary. In 2015 an estimated 54,000 undocumented migrants entered into the nation of 10 million people. In an effort to reduce illegal immigration, Hungary announced in June 2015 that it would construct a 110-mile-long, 12-foot-high fence along its border with Serbia, at a cost of $35 million. The construction of the fence actually increased illicit immigration, as migrants raced to get into the country before the obstacle was completed. Hungary was criticized by other European nations for creating new barriers within Europe, and some argued that the fence might prevent legitimate asylum seekers from being able to seek sanctuary.

Syrian refugees stranded in Hungary in September 2015.

as citizens, but they do have an obligation to ensure that the basic **human rights** of all residents are protected under the United Nations Universal Declaration of Human Rights (1948). For instance, nations have an obligation to provide emergency health care for those who are sick or injured in a manner that is consistent with the access of citizens or legal aliens. Governments also have to grant undocumented migrants access to the justice system to fight exploitation or abuse. As previously discussed, education is another right that most assume is universal.

Ultimately, citizenship provides the most effective method to prevent the exploitation of migrants and assimilate new arrivals into the broader society of any country. However, governments must find an appropriate balance between welcoming new immigrants and protecting their borders against smuggling and other illicit activities.

TEXT-DEPENDENT QUESTIONS

1. How did Spain reduce the number of undocumented immigrants in the country?
2. How much do smugglers charge to transport undocumented immigrants to a new nation?
3. What are examples of human rights of undocumented immigrants?

RESEARCH PROJECTS

1. Research illegal immigration. Write a report that examines the different approaches to reducing the number of undocumented migrants. Which tactic would be the most effective?
2. Research border fences. Create a report on the effectiveness of fences in stopping smuggling or illegal immigration.

FURTHER READING

BOOKS

Chomsky, Aviva. *Undocumented: How Immigration Became Illegal.* Boston: Beacon Press, 2014.

Foner, Mary. *In a New Land: A Comparative View of Immigration.* New York: New York University Press, 2005.

Henke, Holger. *Crossing Over: Comparing Recent Migration in the United States and Europe.* Lanham, MD: Lexington Books, 2005.

Moses, Jonathan W. *International Migration: Globalization's Last Frontier.* London: Zed Books, 2006.

ONLINE

Center for Immigration Studies. http://www.cis.org/.

Klingholz, Reiner. "Immigration Debate: Germany Needs More Foreigners." Spiegel Online International, August 30, 2010. http://www.spiegel.de/international/zeitgeist/immigration-debate-germany-needs-more-foreigners-a-714534.html.

Open Europe. http://www.openeurope.org.uk/.

Pew Research Center. "Remittance Flows Worldwide in 2012." Washington, DC: Pew Research Center, February 20, 2014. http://www.pewsocialtrends.org/2014/02/20/remittance-map/.

Renwick, Danielle, and Brianna Lee. *The U.S. Immigration Debate.* CFR Backgrounder. Washington, DC: Council on Foreign Relations, February 26, 2015. http://www.cfr.org/immigration/us-immigration-debate/p11149.

SERIES GLOSSARY

accountability: making elected officials and government workers answerable to the public for their actions, and holding them responsible for mistakes or crimes.

amnesty: a formal reprieve or pardon for people accused or convicted of committing crimes.

anarchist: a person who believes that government should be abolished because it enslaves or otherwise represses people.

assimilation: the process through which immigrants adopt the cultural, political, and social beliefs of a new nation.

autocracy: a system of government in which a small circle of elites holds most, if not all, political power.

belief: an acceptance of a statement or idea concerning a religion or faith.

citizenship: formal recognition that an individual is a member of a political community.

civil law: statutes and rules that govern private rights and responsibilities and regulate noncriminal disputes over issues such as property or contracts.

civil rights: government-protected liberties afforded to all people in democratic countries.

civil servants: people who work for the government, not including elected officials or members of the military.

corruption: illegal or unethical behavior on the part of officials who abuse their position.

democracy: A government in which the people hold all or most political power and express their preferences on issues through regular voting and elections.

deportation: the legal process whereby undocumented immigrants or those who have violated residency laws are forced to leave their new country.

dual citizenship: being a full citizen of two or more countries.

election: the process of selecting people to serve in public office through voting.

expatriate: someone who resides in a country other than his or her nation of birth.

feminism: the belief in social, economic, and political equality for women.

gender rights: providing access to equal rights for all members of a society regardless of their gender.

glass ceiling: obstacles that prevent the advancement of disadvantaged groups from obtaining senior positions of authority in business, government, and education.

globalization: a trend toward increased interconnectedness between nations and cultures across the world; globalization impacts the spheres of politics, economics, culture, and mass media.

guest workers: citizens of one country who have been granted permission to temporarily work in another nation.

homogenous: a region or nation where most people have the same ethnicity, language, religion, customs, and traditions.

human rights: rights that everyone has, regardless of birthplace or citizenship.

incumbent: an official who currently holds office.

industrialization: the transformation of social life resulting from the technological and economic developments involving factories.

jurisdiction: the official authority to administer justice through activities such as investigations, arrests, and obtaining testimony.

minority: a group that is different—ethnically, racially, culturally, or in terms of religion—within a larger society.

national security: the combined efforts of a country to protect its citizens and interests from harm.

naturalization: the legal process by which a resident noncitizen becomes a citizen of a country.

nongovernmental organization (NGO): a private, nonprofit group that provides services or attempts to influence governments and international organizations.

oligarchy: a country in which political power is held by a small, powerful, but unelected group of leaders.

partisanship: a strong bias or prejudice toward one set of beliefs that often results in an unwillingness to compromise or accept alternative points of view.

refugees: people who are kicked out of their country or forced to flee to another country because they are not welcome or fear for their lives.

right-to-work laws: laws in the United States that forbid making union membership a condition for employment.

secular state: governments that are not officially influenced by religion in making decisions.

sexism: system of beliefs, or ideology, that asserts the inferiority of one sex and justifies discrimination based on gender.

socialist: describes a political system in which major businesses or industries are owned or regulated by the community instead of by individuals or privately owned companies.

socioeconomic status: the position of a person within society, based on the combination of their income, wealth, education, family background, and social standing.

sovereignty: supreme authority over people and geographic space. National governments have sovereignty over their citizens and territory.

theocracy: a system of government in which all major decisions are made under the guidance of religious leaders' interpretation of divine authority.

treason: the betrayal of one's country.

tyranny: rule by a small group or single person.

veto: the ability to reject a law or other measure enacted by a legislature.

wage gap: the disparity in earnings between men and women for their work.

INDEX

ABOUT THE AUTHOR

Tom Lansford is a Professor of Political Science, and a former academic dean, at the University of Southern Mississippi, Gulf Coast. He is a member of the governing board of the National Social Science Association and a state liaison for Mississippi for Project Vote Smart. His research interests include foreign and security policy, and the U.S. presidency. Dr. Lansford is the author, coauthor, editor or coeditor of more than 40 books, and the author of more than one hundred essays, book chapters, encyclopedic entries, and reviews. Recent sole-authored books include: *A Bitter Harvest: U.S. Foreign Policy and Afghanistan* (2003), the *Historical Dictionary of U.S. Diplomacy Since the Cold War* (2007) and *9/11 and the Wars in Afghanistan and Iraq: A Chronology and Reference Guide* (2011). His more recent edited collections include: *America's War on Terror* (2003; second edition 2009), *Judging Bush* (2009), and *The Obama Presidency: A Preliminary Assessment* (2012). Dr. Lansford has served as the editor of the annual *Political Handbook of the World* since 2012.

PHOTO CREDITS